THE
TOWN
OF TURTLE

For Nana Lola: thank you for building our wild,
warm, fun-loving family —M.C.

For refugees, immigrants, and dreamers. For all who
left their countries to find a better home. —C.C.

hmhco.com

The illustrations in this book were done in acrylic, pencil, and paper collage.
The text type was set in Palatino LT Std.
The display type was hand-lettered by Cátia Chien.

Library of Congress Cataloging-in-Publication Data

Names: Cuevas, Michelle, author. | Chien, Cátia, illustrator.
Title: The Town of Turtle / by Michelle Cuevas ; illustrated by Cátia Chien.
Description: Boston ; New York : Houghton Mifflin Harcourt, [2018] | Summary:
Lonely Turtle's only friend is his shadow until he decides to build a
deck, then a garden, then houses and other buildings until, while he naps,
new friends arrive.
Identifiers: LCCN 2016025730 | ISBN 9780544749825 (hardcover)
Subjects: | CYAC: Building—Fiction. | Turtles—Fiction. |
Loneliness—Fiction.
Classification: LCC PZ7.C89268 Tow 2018 | DDC [E]—dc23
LC record available at https://lccn.loc.gov/2016025730

Manufactured in China
SCP 10 9 8 7 6 5 4 3 2 1
4500692815

THE TOWN

OF TURTLE

WORDS BY
Michelle Cuevas

PICTURES BY
Cátia Chien

HOUGHTON MIFFLIN HARCOURT

Boston New York

Turtle lived in a part of the world as empty as a
bird's nest in December.
  Turtle's best (and only) friend was his shadow.
  "Shadow," Turtle would say, looking down. "From
here, you look just like a puddle." Or, "Shadow, is this
the very street where we first met?"
  The shy shadow made no reply.

Needless to say, Turtle spent a lot of
time in his shell. It was very dark inside—as
dark as the inside of a closed flower, as dark
as the underside of a bell.

But in the dark, Turtle dreamed.

Turtle dreamed about a better home. So he decided to make some renovations to his shell.

He started by ordering some paint to brighten his walls.

"I guess I'm sort of . . . green. But not *green* green," said Turtle, looking at paint samples. "Not as bright as grass or lily shoot. But also not as dark as evergreen or, say, envy."

When he finished he had an entire bucket of fern, laurel, and moss green paint left over.

So he decided to build a very small deck, just to use up the extra paint. He employed the use of levers, pulleys, and old-fashioned turtle know-how.

Well, the deck looked just delightful. If he had neighbors, Turtle would have invited them over for a picnic.

But what would they use to toast marshmallows? Perhaps the deck needed a fireplace.

So Turtle built one
of those, too.

The fireplace, Turtle realized,
would need wood.

So he decided to plant a garden with trees.
The garden, he realized, would need a pond.
And the pond, of course, would need lily pads
and a boat dock and a boat.
When he finished, what a view! Turtle realized
there should be houses to enjoy it . . .

. . . so he built some of those as well.

But houses aren't much fun without
other places nearby.

Turtle built a library, and a school,
and an ice-skating rink.

He built a wax museum, an aquarium,
and a Ferris wheel glittering at the top of it all,
among the clouds.
    Turtle kept building until the last drops
of sunlight and paint.

He looked down at his new
shadow and smiled. "Why, Shadow,"
he said, "I hardly recognized you."

After all that work, Turtle needed to take a long nap.

He happened to be an especially deep sleeper. When Turtle slept, he slept the sleep of a broken pocket watch.

He dreamed he had friends who lived in the town he had built.

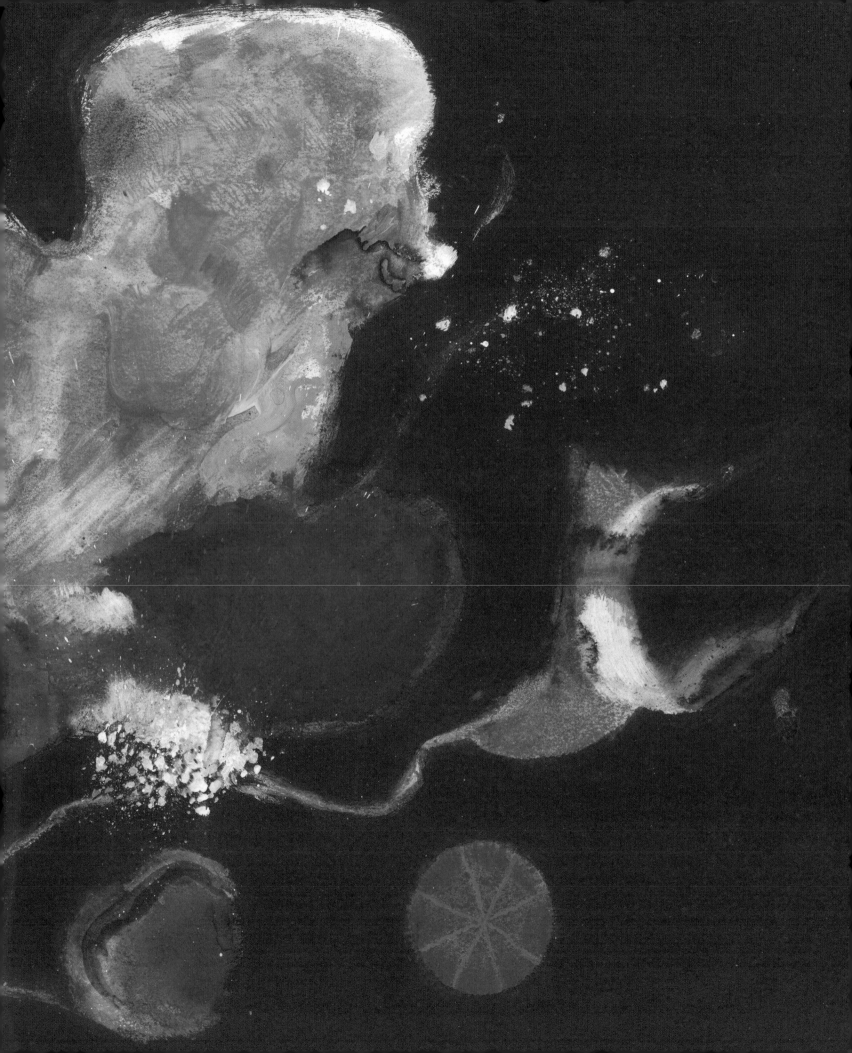

As Turtle slumbered, a peculiar thing happened.

The dream, feeling brave, ventured out into the world. Folks began to gather, speaking in excited hums and whispers.

"What is it?" asked a baker.

"Looks like the most beautiful town," said an inventor.

"A town just waiting to be moved into," said a mailman.

And you know what?

That's just what they did.

A painter, a sailor, and a ballerina came first.

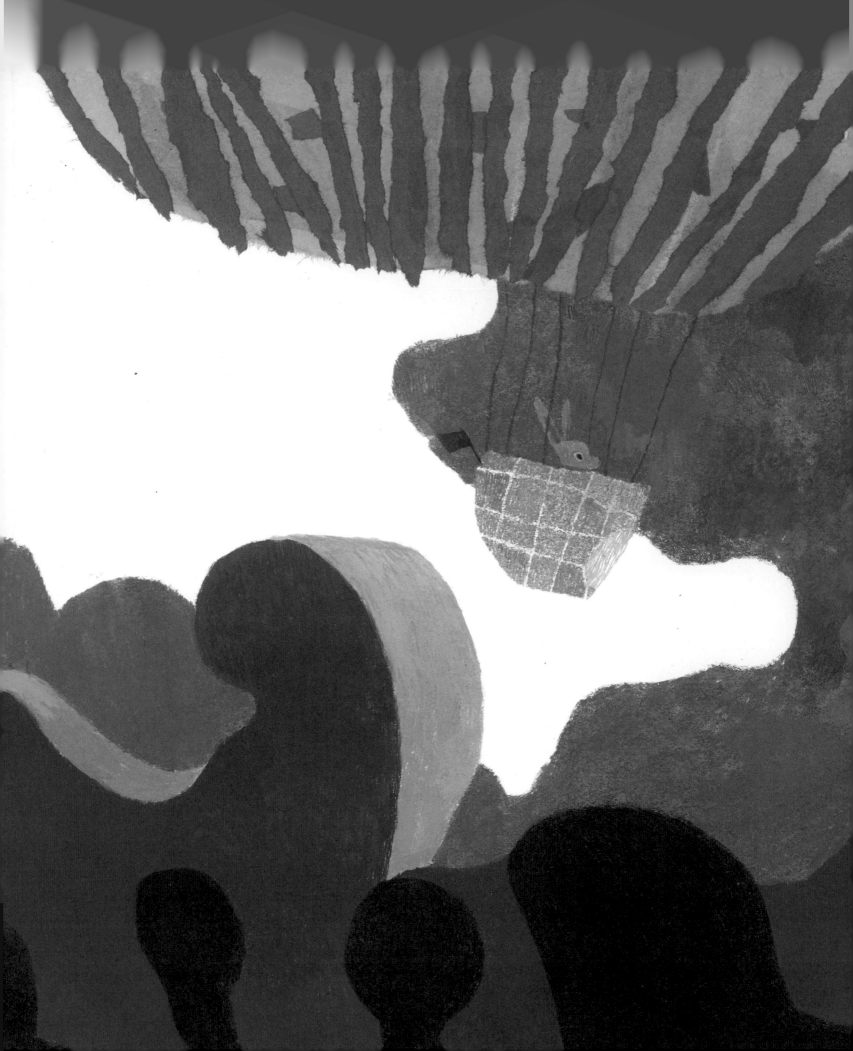

Then a topiarist, a hot-air balloonist,
and one tightrope-riding unicyclist.

The wind moved into the trees, laughter moved into the houses, and light moved into the dark.

When Turtle finally awoke
from his long, long nap, he was
shocked. But also delighted.

Sometimes, thought Turtle,
the world you dream can come
alive all around you.

That night, when Turtle was tucked cozy
into his shell, he called out to his town.
He called good night to the painter.
Good night to the sailor.

Good night to the ballerina, the mailman,
the inventor, the baker.
   Good night to the one tightrope-riding
unicyclist.

Good night to the wind, and the laughter, and the light.

Good night to everyone, everyone
in the Town of Turtle.